HELP!

D1538186

THE PIRATE HAS LOST HIS SHIPMATES!

I had **sixteen** shipmates, now I have **none**...

I went to find treasure; now they've all **gone**!

Forgive me for such a silly blunder.

Where could they be, I wonder...?

SALTY SAM

I really need him in my crew.
I wonder where he's gotten to?!

GRIBBLE

He looks after my parrot for me...
but he's gone missing.
Where could he be?

SKIPPER SCARLET

She loves to **shock and scare**.
It's a pirate's life for Scarlet,
can you **find her anywhere?!**

FLYNN

He loves a sword fight.
Please help... he's vanished
out of sight!

BEARDY JOE

He likes to eat, but he loves to drink.
Let's find him, what do you think?

SEAWORTHY SID

He scrubs the deck then washes all
the clothes. Where has he got to?
Nobody knows!

DANGER
SLIPPERY ICE!

PEGGY LEG

I know she must be around...
but, I wonder, can she be found?

BARNACLE BILL

He sleeps all day then works all night... but not anymore, he's vanished out of sight!

MARTY MCGEE

He walked the plank and **never came back**... his shirt is red and his **shorts are black**!

LADY SWASHBUCKLE

She knows everything there is to know. I wonder where she's **decided to go?**

MR SCURVY

HARRY HOOK

These two love to hunt for
treasure and gold.
They're somewhere here,
so I'm told!

PENNY PINCHER

She joined the ship last week,
she's really quite new.
Where could she be? I haven't got a clue!

SKULL N' BONES

The twins have **abandoned ship**.
I wonder where they went on
their trip...?

TIMBERS

This pirate is really quite kind.
Please help; she's the
last one to find!

THANK YOU!

Everyone has been found!
and here they are,

all safe and sound!

A **bonus** search!

PIRATE SKULLS!

The three above are hiding in the book. Don't believe me? Go take a look!

THE END!

HELP! BOOKS

Find us on Amazon!

Discover all of the titles available in the series; including these below...

HELP! MY MONSTERS ARE ON THE LOOSE!

HELP! MY DINOSAURS ARE LOST IN THE CITY!

HELP! THERE'S AN ANIMAL THIEF ON THE LOOSE!

HELP! MY HALLOWEEN FRIENDS ARE MISSING!

HELP! MY ROBOTS ARE LOST IN THE CITY!

HELP! I NEED MY SUPERHEROES!

Made in the USA
Middletown, DE
03 August 2020